For Lili, Gina, Poopy
and the little one to come

So, here you are, house three-forty-four,
a strange, little spaceman that's knocked on my door.
I knew that you'd come, I knew it too well
and I already don't like you, I bet you can tell.
The reason I don't? Well, that's simple to see.
After all, you're an alien, you're different than me.

I know what you're up to, your plan is unfurled.
You've flown here by spaceship to take over the world.
What else do you want from us? What are your demands?
You evil, little creature from far off lands.
We won't be escaping. There's nowhere to hide.
Your U Flying Object has been i - dentified.

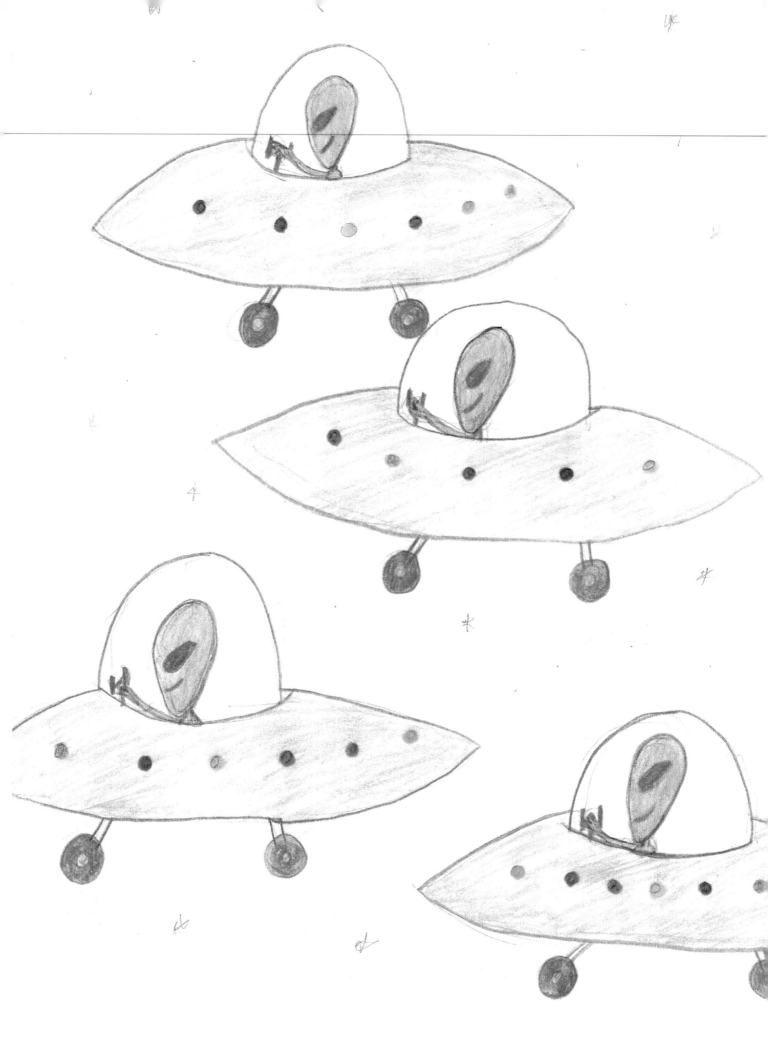

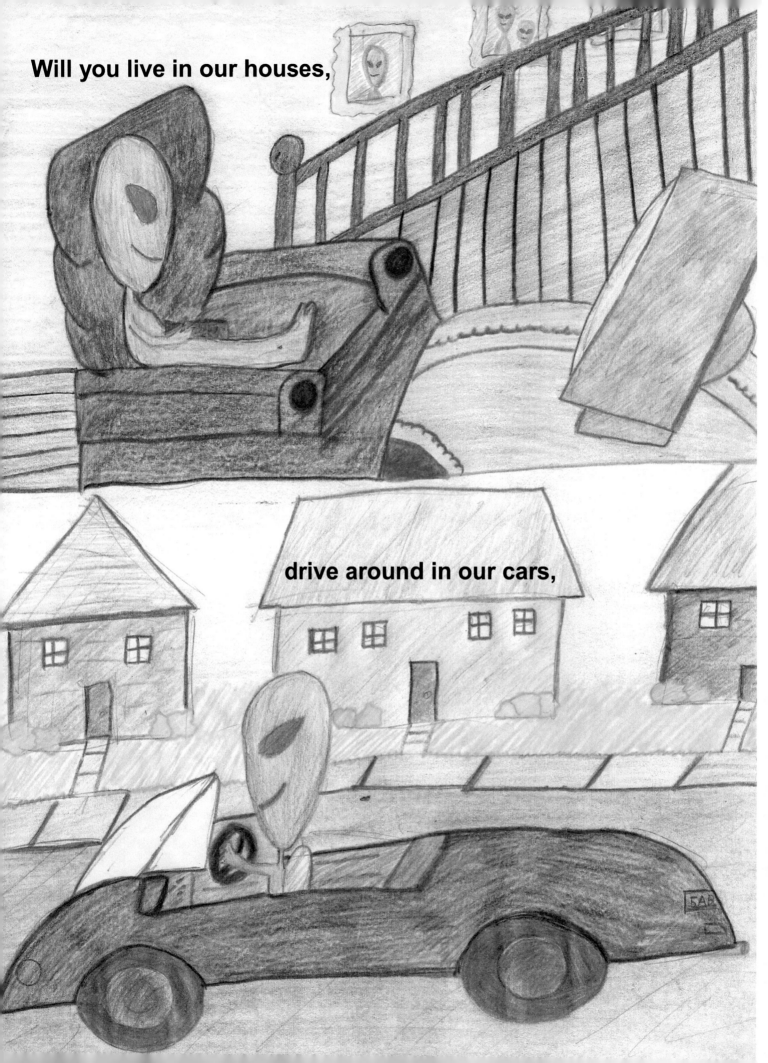

or pack everything up and take it back to the stars?

Do you want JUST our planet?
Are WE under attack?
Are you all really hungry
and I'm your first human snack?

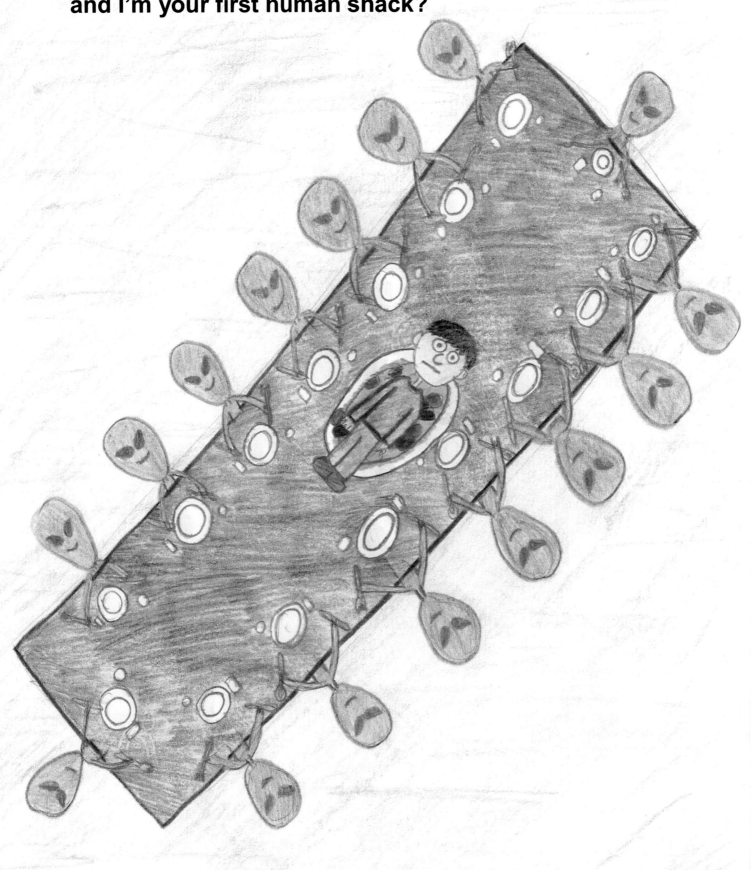

Will you chew us to pieces?
Will you swallow us whole?

Will you bathe in our
bathtubs
and eat all our food…

and make all our stuff your stuff?

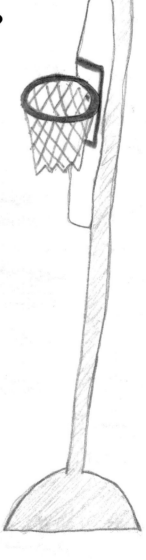

(…which is really quite rude.)

…and legs, extra short.

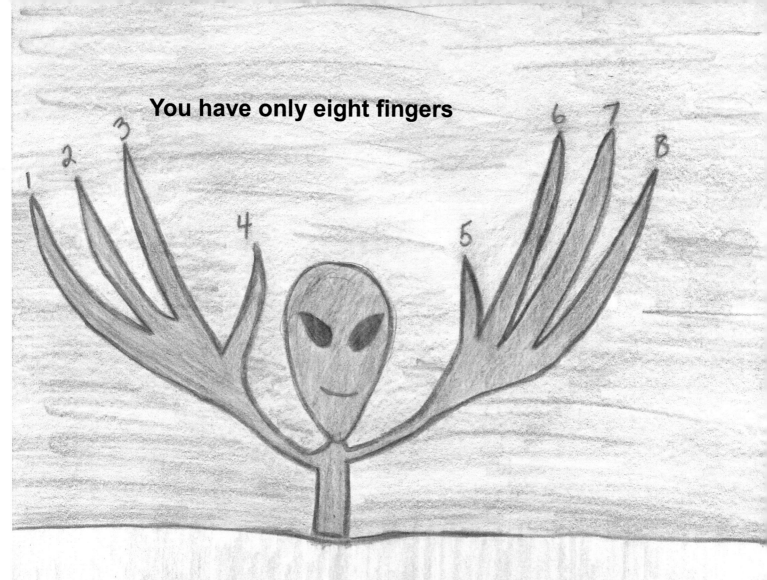

Here to blow up my planet without one single care.
Get back in your spaceship and take to the air!
Can't you just go? Can't you just leave me be?!?
After all, you're a monster, you're different than me!

I have stood here and listened to all that you've said
as you spoke of my skin and my extra large head.
Well, there you were right, but let me explain…
In my extra large head there's an oversized brain.
And so, my fine fellow with legs twice as long,
I feel I must tell you that you're really quite wrong.

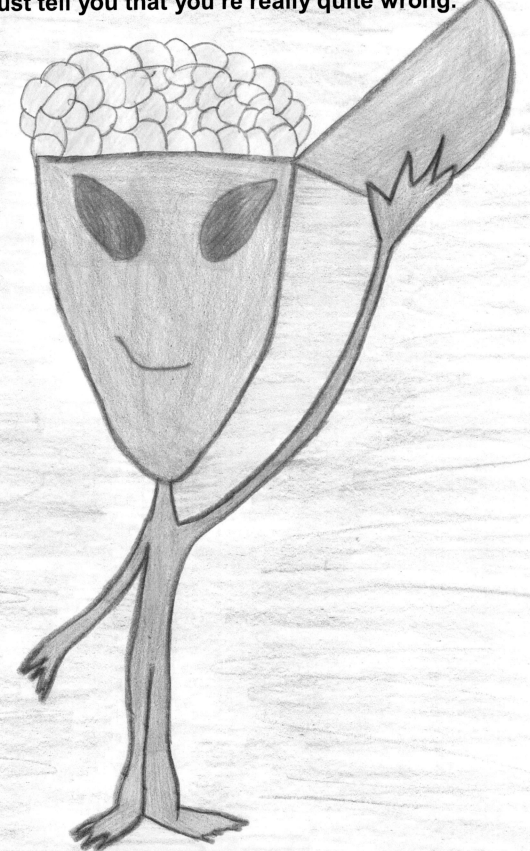

There were no sorts of lasers on spaceships I've flown.

I don't want your belongings. I have stuff of my own.

Planet Earth truly is a very lovely place
but I have no plans of taking it back with me into space.

I would never want a person, whole or not, inside my belly!

My favorite foods are pizza
and peanut butter and grape jelly.

Where did you hear these rumors?
Do they really seem like me?
Did you see them in the movies?
Did you watch them on T.V.?

I like nature and music and sports and apple pie.
If you'd only get to know me you'd see I'm really quite a guy.

And I AM wearing clothing, with pre-attached boots, but on my planet we all wear skin-styled suits. They're colored just like us and fit, oh so well, that whether we're dressed or not, you really can't tell.

You've only just met me and yet, hold a grudge.
You're too hasty to hate me. You're too quick to judge.
If you don't see it now, then you're sure to see later
that my family and I are not space invaders.

Our planet had grown dark.
Our planet was cold.
It was time to get moving.
Our old house was sold.

We needed a new start, a new place to stay,
so together we cruised through the whole Milky Way.

We searched for a home and the house that we picked was the house next to your house, house three-forty-six.

It's true that there are differences between aliens and men
but they aren't any reason why we two can't be friends.
You may be an Earthling and I come from the stars
but it doesn't matter what we look like, it matters who we are.

About the Author

 Anthony S. Bilotti is a high school teacher of Italian. He is also the singer, songwriter, and guitarist for the amazing indie-rock band, Bluish. He still skateboards (yes, still) and is an impressive juggler. He enjoys fielding ground balls, building Rube-Goldberg machines, and is fascinated by astronomy. He was born and raised in the forgotten borough of Staten Island, New York where he still lives, hiking, biking and having adventures with his wife and three amazing kids. He also has a remarkably well-kept chinstrap beard.

Ryan,
Enjoy the book!

Made in the USA
Middletown, DE
10 November 2023

42391031R00024